ROSCO VS. THE BABY

LINDSAY WARD

Simon & Schuster Books for Young Readers

New York London Toronto Sydney New Delhi

SIMON & SCHUSTER BOOKS FOR YOUNG READERS · An imprint of Simon & Schuster Children's Publishing Division · 1230 Avenue of the Americas, New York, New York 10020

SIMON & SCHUSTER BOOKS FOR YOUNG READERS is a trademark of Simon & Schuster, Inc.

For information about special discounts for bulk purchases, please contact Simon & Schuster Special Sales at 1-866-506-1949 or business@simonandschuster.com.

The Simon & Schuster Speakers Bureau can bring authors to your live event. For more information or to book an event, contact the
Simon & Schuster Speakers Bureau at 1-866-248-3049 or visit our website at www.simonspeakers.com.

Book design by Lucy Ruth Cummins · The text for this book is set in Futura. · The illustrations for this book are rendered in in cut paper, watercolor, and pencil.

Manufactured in China · 0316 SCP · 10 9 8 7 6 5 4 3 2 1 · Library of Congress Cataloging-in-Publication Data

Ward, Lindsay, author, illustrator. · Rosco vs. the baby / Lindsay Ward.—1st edition. · pages cm

Summary: Rosco the dog is the undisputed heavyweight champ of his home, with something to say—loudly—about everything until the baby arrives,
making at least as much noise and getting all of the attention that was once Rosco's, and the championship bout begins.

ISBN 978-1-4814-3657-1 (hardcover) · ISBN 978-1-4814-3658-8 (eBook) · [1. Dogs—Fiction. 2. Babies—Fiction. 3. Human-animal relationships—Fiction.
4. Humorous stories.] I. Title. II. Title: Rosco versus the baby. · PZ7.W214316Ros 2015 · [E]—dc23 · 2014040896

For Steph—L. W.

NO CATS!!!

ROSCO'S TOYS

KEEP OUT

Everybody knew Rosco.
He was the heavyweight champ
of 17 Parkwood Avenue.
All day, every day, Rosco sat
on the front porch
watching . . .
waiting . . .
and then . . .

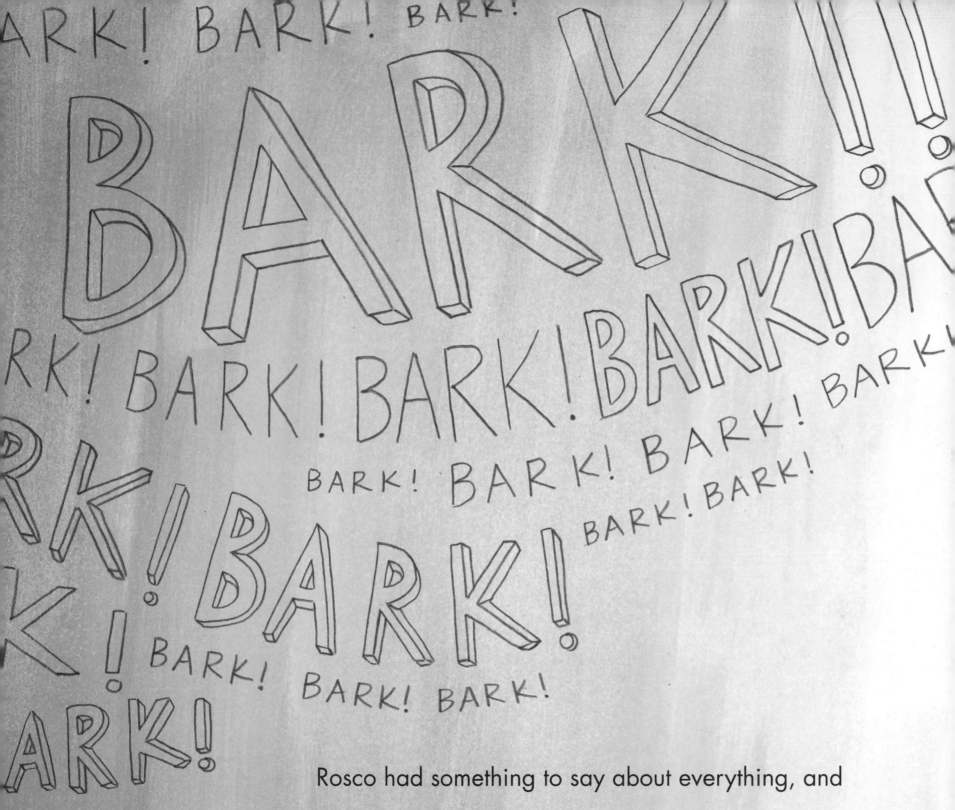

Rosco had something to say about everything, and nothing was louder than Rosco.

Until the day the baby arrived.

Rosco noticed a funny smell right away.

Something wasn't right. . . .

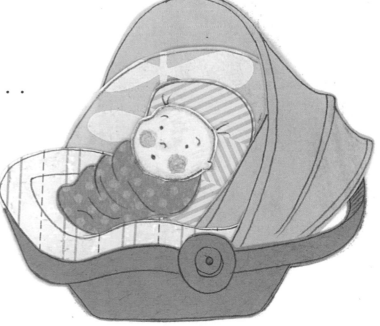

Rosco stopped barking. The baby stopped crying.

Rosco glared at the baby.

THE BABY

S.

The baby glared at Rosco.

This house wasn't big enough for the both of them.

Soon things began to change. . . .

Rosco didn't eat first, the baby did.

Rosco didn't nap with his buddy,

the baby did.

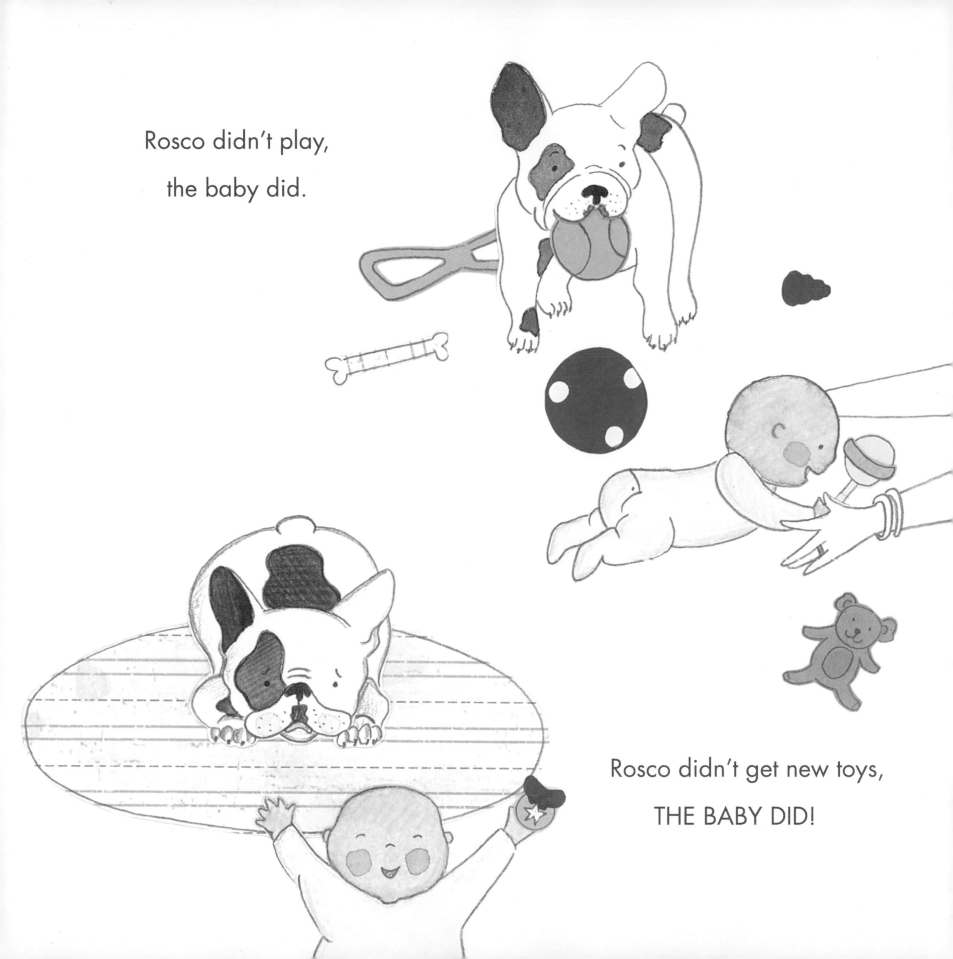

Rosco didn't play,
the baby did.

Rosco didn't get new toys,
THE BABY DID!

The baby meant business. But so did Rosco.

THE BABY

S.

Two heavyweights. One house.

During a garage sale,

Rosco put out a special item.

One afternoon, Rosco played hide-and-seek . . . with the baby.

Then in the middle of the night, Rosco left a surprise.

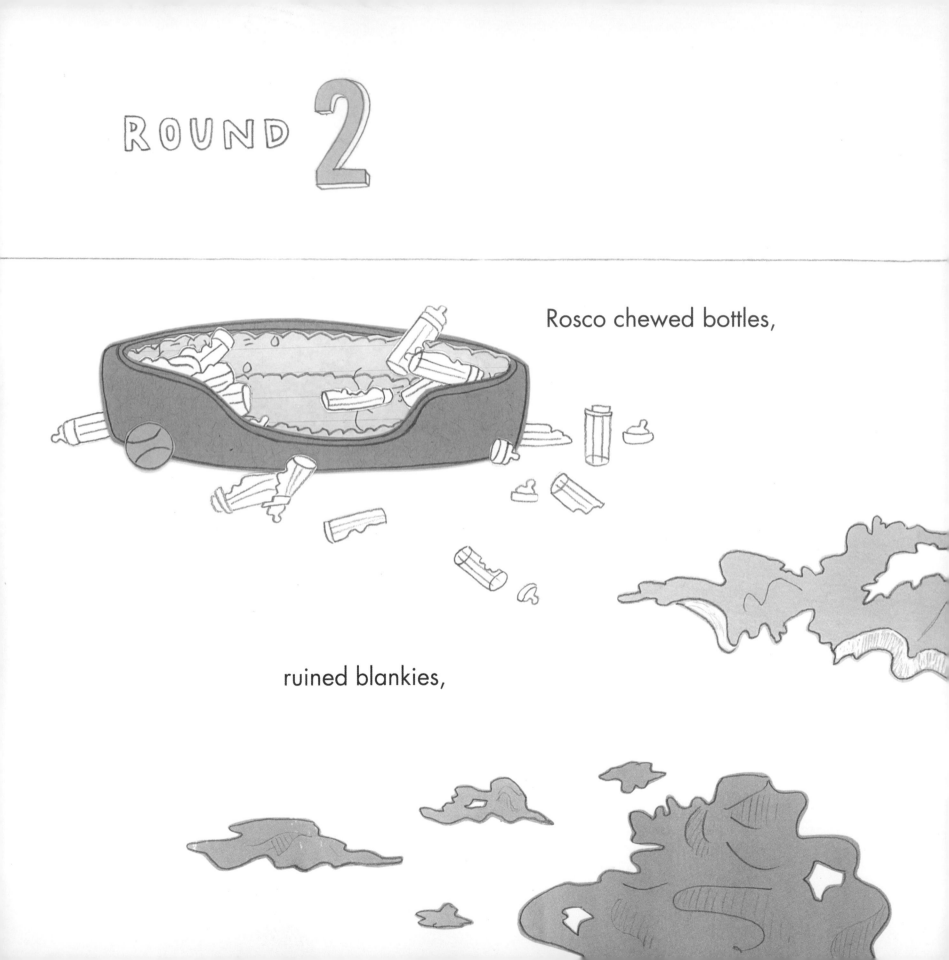

ROUND 2

Rosco chewed bottles,

ruined blankies,

and howled during nap time.

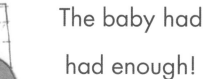

The baby had

had enough!

ROUND 3

When Rosco was playing outside,

the baby made mud pies . . .

on Rosco.

When Rosco ate dinner,

the baby hid his toys.

When Rosco went for a walk, the baby threw out

his favorite ball.

The green one.

With the fuzzy spots.

ROSCO
2

THE BABY
1

And so it went. Rosco vs. the Baby.

Day after day. Month after month.

ROUND 4

The Baby Bottom.

ROUND **5** The Four-Leg Drop.

ROUND **6** The Pile Driver.

ROUND **7**

The Slobber Knocker.

ROUND **8**...

Finally, they were totally

knocked out.

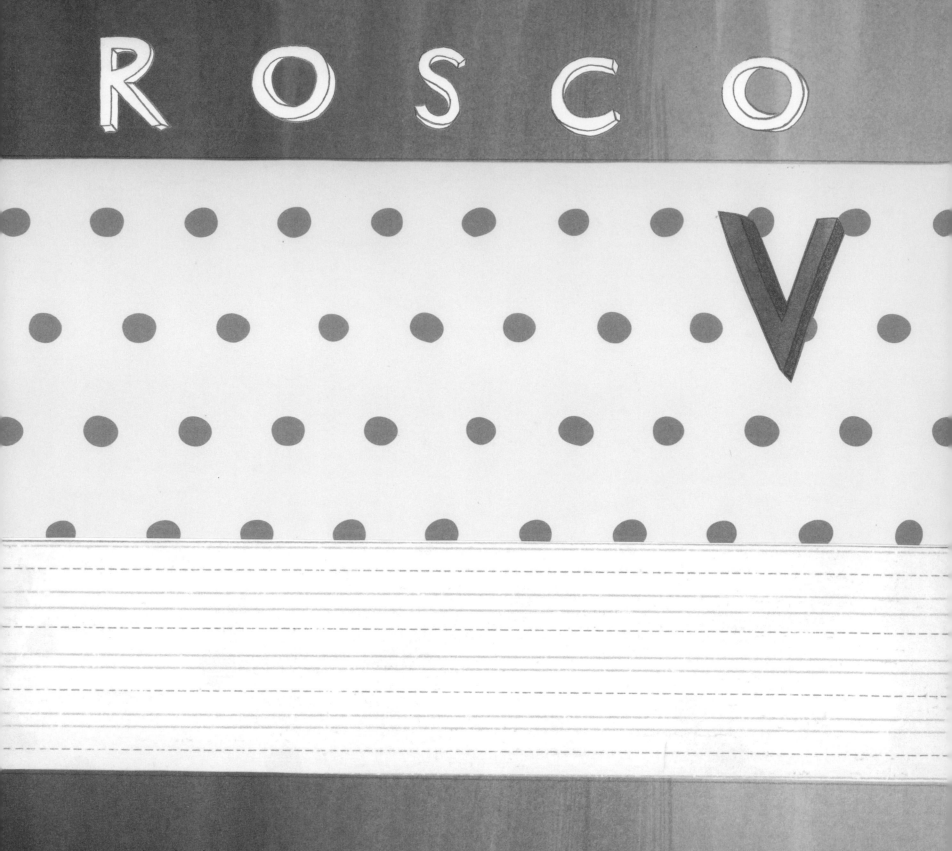

The baby stared at Rosco. Rosco stared at the baby. Hmmmm . . .

THE BABY

S.

The baby smiled at Rosco. Rosco smiled at the baby.

!BARK! BARK!

ARK! BARK! BARK! BARK!

RK! BARK! BARK! BARK! BA

K! BARK! BARK! BARK!

BARK! BARK! BARK!

BARK!

Soon things began to change. Again.

Rosco and the baby became inseparable.

Then it happened. . . .

Rosco looked at the baby. The baby looked at Rosco.

They glared at the new babies. Together.